W9-AGP-117

Hansel and Gretel

First published in the United States by
Larousse & Co., Inc.
572 Fifth Avenue
New York, N.Y. 10036
1983

This edition first published in Denmark by
Gyldendalske Boghandel as *Hans og Grete* in 1983

Illustrations Copyright © 1982 Svend Otto S.
English Translation Copyright © 1983 Pelham Books Ltd

ISBN 0-88332-291-9
Library of Congress Catalog card No. 82-083826

Printed in Denmark

GRIMM
Hansel and Gretel

Illustrated by Svend Otto S.

Translated by Anthea Bell

Larousse & Co., Inc. *New York*

There was once a poor woodcutter who lived just outside a great forest with his wife and his two children. The boy was called Hansel and the girl Gretel. The woodcutter and his family had little to eat and drink, and when hard times came to that part of the country he could not even get their daily bread.

As he lay in bed one evening thinking, tossing and turning in his anxiety, he sighed and said to his wife, "What will become of us? How can we feed our poor children when we have nothing left for ourselves?"

"I'll tell you what to do, husband," said she. "Early tomorrow morning we will take the children out into the depths of the forest. We'll light them a fire, and give them each a piece of bread, and then we'll go to our work and leave them alone there. They'll never find their way home again, and we shall be rid of them."

"No, wife!" said the woodcutter. "I'll do no such thing! How could I bring myself to leave my children alone in the forest, where the wild beasts would soon come and tear them to pieces?"

"You fool!" she said. "Then we shall all four die of hunger, and you might as well plane the planks for our coffins smooth at once!" And she would give him no peace until he agreed. "But I feel sorry for the poor children," said her husband.

Now the two children were so hungry that they had not been able to sleep either, and they heard what their stepmother said to their father. Gretel wept bitterly. "It's all up with us now!" she said to Hansel.

"Hush, Gretel," said Hansel. "Don't worry. I'll think of some way to help us."

And when the woodcutter and his wife were asleep he got up,

put on his clothes, unlatched the door and slipped out. It was bright moonlight, and the white pebbles lying outside the house shone like silver pennies. Hansel bent down and filled his pocket with all the pebbles it would hold. Then he went in again, and told Gretel, "Cheer up, little sister, and go to sleep. God will not abandon us!" And he lay down in bed again.

Early next morning, before the sun was up, the woman came and woke the two children. "Get up, lazybones!" she said. "We're going into the forest to chop wood." And she gave them each a piece of bread, saying, "There, that's for your dinner, but mind you don't eat it before noon, for you'll get no more."

Gretel put both pieces of bread under her apron, because Hansel's pocket was full of pebbles, and then they all set off along the path into the forest together.

When they had been walking for a while, Hansel stopped and looked back at the house. He did this again and again.

"Why do you keep looking back and lagging behind, Hansel?" asked his father. "Come along, pick your feet up!"

"Oh, Father," said Hansel, "I'm just looking at my little white cat sitting up on the roof, saying goodbye to me."

"Silly child!" said the woman. "That's not your little cat, it's the morning sun shining on the chimney."

However, Hansel had not been looking back at the cat. He had been dropping the shiny pebbles from his pocket on the path, one by one.

When they were in the middle of the forest, their father said, "Now, children, gather wood and I'll light you a fire to keep you warm."

Hansel and Gretel gathered a little pile of brushwood. The fire was lit, and when the flames were blazing up the woman said, "Now, children, lie down by the fire and rest. We're going on into the forest to chop wood, and when we've finished we'll come back for you."

Hansel and Gretel sat by the fire, and when noon came they ate their pieces of bread. They could hear the sound of the woodcutter's axe, and so they thought their father was nearby. However, it was not really his axe, but a branch he had tied to a dead tree, so that the wind blew it to and fro.

When they had been sitting there for a long time, the children were so tired that their eyes closed and they fell asleep. And when at last they woke, it was dark night.

Gretel began to cry. "How shall we ever get out of this forest?" she said. But Hansel comforted her. "Just wait a little, until the moon is up, and then we'll find our way!"

And when the full moon had risen, Hansel took his little sister's hand and they followed the pebbles, which shone like newly minted silver and showed them the way.

They walked all night, and at dawn they came to their father's house. They knocked at the door, and when the woman opened it and saw Hansel and Gretel she said, "Oh, you naughty children! Why did you sleep in the forest so long? We thought you were never coming home!" However, their father was overjoyed, for it had gone to his heart to leave them alone there.

Not long afterwards hard times came again, and the children heard their stepmother talking to their father in bed at night. "We have eaten everything," she said. "All we have left is half a loaf of bread, and when that is finished there'll be nothing. The children must go. We'll take them even farther into the forest, so that they can never find their way out again. If we don't do that there's no hope for us."

Her husband was very sad, and he thought: it would be better to share my last crust with my children. But his wife would not listen to anything he said.

She was angry, and scolded him. A man who has said "A" must

say "B" too, and since he had given way to her once, he had to give way again.

But the children were lying awake, and had heard all that was said. When the woodcutter and his wife were asleep, Hansel got up again to go out and pick up pebbles, as he had done before. But the woman had locked the door, and Hansel could not get out. However, he comforted his little sister and said, "Don't cry, Gretel. Go to sleep. I'm sure the good Lord will help us!"

Early next morning the woman came and got the children out of bed. She gave them each a piece of bread, even smaller than the

last time. On their way to the forest Hansel crumbled the bread in his pocket, and he kept stopping to drop a crumb on the ground.

"Why are you standing there looking back, Hansel?" asked his father. "Come along!"

"I'm looking at my little dove sitting on the roof, saying goodbye to me," said Hansel.

"Silly child!" said the woman. "That's not your little dove, it's the morning sun shining on the chimney."

Bit by bit, however, Hansel scattered all his crumbs on the ground.

The woman led the children still deeper into the forest, where they had never been in all their lives before. A big fire was lit again, and their stepmother said, "Just sit there, children, and when you're tired you can sleep a little. We're going on into the forest to chop wood, and in the evening, when we've finished, we'll come back for you."

At noon Gretel shared her piece of bread with Hansel, because he had scattered his along the way. Then they went to sleep, and evening came and went, but no one fetched the poor children. They did not wake until it was dark night. Hansel comforted his little sister and said, "Wait until the moon rises, Gretel. Then we'll see the crumbs of bread I scattered, and they will show us the way home."

When the moon rose they set off, but they did not find a single crumb, for all the thousands of birds who flew about the forest and the fields had pecked them up. "I'm sure we'll find our way," Hansel told Gretel. But they did not.

They walked all night until morning, and then they walked all day until evening, but they could not find their way out of the forest, and they were very hungry, for they had nothing to eat but the few berries they could find. Then, since they were so tired that their legs would not carry them any farther, they lay down under a tree and went to sleep.

Morning came: the third morning since they had left their father's house. Once again they began to walk, but they kept going deeper into the forest, and if they did not soon get help they would surely die.

When noon came, they saw a beautiful snow-white bird sitting on a branch, singing so beautifully that they stopped to listen.

And when it had finished singing, it flapped its wings and flew on ahead of them. They followed until they came to a little house.

The bird settled on the roof. When the children came closer, they saw that the house was built of bread and roofed with cake, and the windows were made of barley-sugar.

"Let's set to and have a good meal!" said Hansel. "I'll take a piece of the roof, and you can eat part of a window, Gretel; it will be nice and sweet."

So Hansel reached up and broke off a little of the roof, to see how it tasted, and Gretel began nibbling at the window panes.

Then they heard a shrill voice inside the house:

"Nibble, nibble, mousie,
Who's nibbling at my housie?"

The children answered:

"Heaven's child,
The wind so wild."

And they went on eating, undisturbed. Hansel, who thought the roof tasted very good, broke off a larger piece of it, and Gretel pushed out a whole round window pane and sat down to enjoy it.

Suddenly the door opened, and an old, old woman hobbled out, leaning on a stick. Hansel and Gretel were so frightened that they dropped what they were holding. However, the old woman nodded her head, and said, "Why, dear children, who brought you here? Come in and stay with me, and no harm will come to you." She took them both by the hand and led them into her little house. She gave them good food and drink: milk and sweet pancakes, apples and nuts. Afterwards, she showed them two pretty little beds made up with white sheets, and Hansel and Gretel lay down and thought they were in Paradise.

But the old woman was only pretending to be kind. She was really a wicked witch, who lay in wait for children, and she had built the house made of bread and cake just to lure them to her. When she had a child in her clutches she would kill it, cook it and eat it, and that was a feast-day for her.

Witches have red eyes and cannot see very far, but they have keen noses like animals, and they can tell when humans are close. So when Hansel and Gretel came near, the witch smiled a wicked smile and said gleefully, "I've caught them now, and they won't escape me!"

Early next morning, before the children were awake, she got up, and when she looked at them lying there so peacefully, with their plump pink cheeks, she said to herself, "Ah, they'll make a tasty dish!"

Then she took Hansel in her bony hands, and locked him in a hutch with a barred door. He could shout all he liked, but it did him no good.

After that she went to Gretel, shook her awake, and said, "Get up, you lazy girl, and cook your brother something good! He's out in the hutch, and I shall fatten him up. When he's nice and fat I'll eat him."

Gretel began to weep bitterly, but it was no use: she had to do as the wicked witch said.

So poor Hansel had the very best of food, while Gretel got nothing but crayfish shells. Every morning the old woman would hobble out to the hutch and say, "Stick your finger through the bars, Hansel, and let me feel if you're getting fat."

But Hansel put a bone through the bars. The old woman, with her poor eyesight, could not see it and thought it was his finger.

She wondered why he never got any fatter, and when four weeks had passed and Hansel was still thin, she lost patience and decided not to wait any longer.

"Now then, Gretel," she told the girl, "hurry up and fetch water. Whether Hansel is fat or whether he's thin, I shall kill him and cook him tomorrow!"

How Hansel's poor little sister wept as she fetched the water, and how the tears ran down her cheeks!

"Dear God, please help us!" she prayed. "Oh, if only the wild beasts had eaten us in the forest, then at least we'd have died together."

"Never mind your crying," said the old woman, "that won't help you."

Early next morning Gretel had to go out, fill a great cauldron with water and light the fire.

"But first we'll bake bread," said the old woman. "I've heated the oven and kneaded the dough." And she made poor Gretel go over to the oven, where the flames were already blazing up.

"Crawl in," said the witch, "and see if it's hot enough. Then we can put the bread in."

Once Gretel was inside, however, the witch was going to close the oven door and leave her roasting. Then she meant to eat her. But Gretel guessed what her plan was, and said, "Oh, I don't know how to do that. How do I get into the oven?"

"Silly goose!" said the old woman. "The oven door is big enough – look, I could get in myself!" And she came hobbling up and stuck her own head in the oven. Then Gretel gave her such a push that the rest of her went in too. Gretel slammed the iron door and latched it shut.

Oh, how horribly the old woman began to yell! But Gretel ran away, and the wicked witch was left to perish miserably.

As for Gretel, she ran straight to Hansel, opened the door of his hutch and cried, "Hansel, we're safe, and the old witch is dead!"

Then Hansel jumped up like a bird let out of its cage.

How happy the children were as they hugged and kissed each other and jumped for joy! Now that there was nothing more to fear, they went into the witch's house and found chests full of pearls and jewels standing everywhere.

"These are better than pebbles," said Hansel, and he filled his pockets with all they would hold.

"I want to take something home too," said Gretel, and she filled her apron with jewels.

"Now," said Hansel, "let's go, and leave this witch's wood behind!"

However, when they had been walking for some time they came to a wide stretch of water.

"We can't get across," said Hansel. "I see no bridge or plank."

"And there's no ferry to take us over," said Gretel, "but there is a duck swimming on the water. If I ask her, she will help us across."

So she called out:

> "Hansel and Gretel stand on the bank,
> Little duck, help we lack.
> We have no bridge, we have no plank.
> Carry us over on your white back!"

Sure enough, the duck swam over to them. Hansel sat on her
back, and told his sister to join him.

"No," said Gretel, "we'd be too heavy for the duck. She will
take us over one at a time."

And so the good duck did. When they were safely across the
water, and had been walking for some time, the forest began to
look more and more familiar to them, and at last they saw their
father's house in the distance. Then they began to run. They
rushed inside and flung their arms round their father's neck.

The poor man had not had a moment's peace of mind since he left the children in the forest. As for his wife, she was dead. Gretel shook out her apron, so that the pearls and jewels flew about the room, and Hansel brought more of them out of his pocket in handfuls. All their troubles were over now, and they lived happily together.

My story is over – and there goes a mouse! Catch her if you can, and you may make a fur cap of her.